by Amanda Brandon

Illustrated by Catalina Echeverri

A Knit and a Knot

Granny Mutton was teaching Little Lionel to knit.

"Knit one, purl one, knit one, purl one,

WHOOPS! Drop one."

He twisted and looped the wool around the needles.

He was knitting squares to make a blanket.

"This blanket will have more knots than knits."

Lionel held them up for Granny to see.

"Keep going, you're doing well," she said. "Let's use my squishy, squashy, red wool."

They looked high
and they looked low but they couldn't find it.

"Bother, my lovely new wool has disappeared."

"Don't worry, I'll find it," Little Lionel said,
"I will solve the mystery of the missing wool."

He put on his detective outfit and set off from Granny's house.

He saw Rocky the sheep-dog at the gate.

"Granny has lost her wool and I'm looking for clues."

"I'll help," Rocky barked. "Look! There's some red wool on the hedge."

Little Lionel tried to grab it but the wool suddenly disappeared. He fell in the prickly hedge.

"Ouch! Someone pulled that wool from me. There must be a thief in the farmyard."

"Quick," Rocky said. "After them!"

They raced after the wool.

They heard a rumble behind them...
An angry bull sniffed and snorted.

Little Lionel shouted, "I detect BIG trouble!"
They both leapt over the fence...

"Now we've lost the trail," Lionel said, disappointed.

"Not yet." Rocky pointed to footprints on the path.

They sploshed across the muddy farmyard
to follow the **tiny** prints.

Little Lionel saw the end of the wool peek
from a hole in the barn door.

They had found the thief.

They pulled the wool.

Someone tugged the other end...

They pulled again and the wool whizzed over their heads.

"H-E-L-P!"

The thief cried as he spun round and dropped into a big pile of straw.

Rocky and Lionel
dived to the rescue...

"Pipsqueak!" they cried in surprise. "Why did you take Granny's wool?"

"I'm sorry. I wanted cosy wool to make a bed for my new brothers and sisters."

"You'll have to give it back,"
Little Lionel said.
"But don't worry, I have just
the thing instead..."

He fetched his knitting and sang,

"Make a square with a knit and a knot

to create the perfect mouse's cot,"
and he gently tucked
a mouse under each
patchwork piece.

Pipsqueak, Rocky and Lionel returned the wool to Granny Mutton.

"Thank you Pipsqueak, you're just in time..." she said.

"Just in time for what?" Pipsqueak asked as she handed them some needles each.

"To start a new knitting club."